For Violet Nymphadora

BLOOMSBURY CHILDREN'S BOOKS
Bloomsbury Publishing Plc
50 Bedford Square, London, WC1B 3DP, UK

BLOOMSBURY, BLOOMSBURY CHILDREN'S BOOKS and the Diana logo are
trademarks of Bloomsbury Publishing Plc

First published in Great Britain 2020 by Bloomsbury Publishing Plc

A catalogue record for this book is available from the British Library

ISBN: HB: 978-1-5266-0720-1, PB: 978-1-5266-0719-5, eBook: 978-1-5266-1057-7

2 4 6 8 10 9 7 5 3 1 (hardback), 2 4 6 8 10 9 7 5 3 1 (paperback)

Printed and bound in China by Leo Paper Products, Heshan, Guangdong

All papers used by Bloomsbury Plc are natural, recyclable products from wood grown in well managed forests.
The manufacturing process conform to the environmental regulations of the country of origin

To find out more about our authors and books visit www.bloomsbury.com and sign up for our newsletters
To find out more about Katie Abey visit www.katieabey.co.uk

WE CATCH THE BUS

KATIE ABEY

BLOOMSBURY
CHILDREN'S BOOKS
LONDON OXFORD NEW YORK NEW DELHI SYDNEY

We Catch the Bus

Which bus would you catch?

We Ride Emergency Vehicles

Choose your **favourite** animal. What are they doing?

We Ride Tractors

What are the animals **doing** on the farm?

Who is hiding in the pond?

Ploughing soil

Moving logs

I ♥ tractors

My vehicle is red

Cutting the grass

Camping

We Fly Rockets

The animals have blasted off! What will they **find** in space?